Mālie the Manō

Written by
Courtnie Tokuda

Illustrated by
Anneth Lagamo

ISLAND HERITAGE™
PUBLISHING
A DIVISION OF THE MADDEN CORPORATION

Mālie the *manō* was terribly shy,
so timid in nature and no one knew why.

For my daughters, Cerenity and Taylor
~C.T.

"No act of kindness, no matter how small, is ever wasted." (Aesop)
~A.L.

ISLAND HERITAGE™
PUBLISHING
A DIVISION OF THE MADDEN CORPORATION

94-411 Kō'aki Street
Waipahu, Hawai'i 96797-2806
Orders: (800) 468-2800
Information: (808) 564-8800
Fax: (808) 564-8877
welcometotheislands.com
COP 192404

ISBN: 1-61710-398-5
First Edition, Second Printing—2019

She never was crafty, or cunning or mean
Mālie preferred to be calm and serene.

While other *manō* in the ocean craved meat,
Mālie preferred to have seaweed to eat.
Her cousins and brothers would circle around,
Discussing her faults and the reasons they found.

"Perhaps she's part *honu*," one cousin suggested.
"*Honu's* more fearsome," her brother contested.
They laughed at her loudly with wide open jaws.
They jeered at her nature and pondered the cause.

She swam off embarrassed and circled the reef.
She tried to come up with an end to her grief.
"Mālie!" The call made her turn with a cry
as Niuhi, one of her cousins swam by

Niuhi was striking and stunning and vain.
"I'll tell you what's wrong. It's simple and plain.
Mālie, you're weak. You're dull and so slow.
I know that it hurts, but you just need to know.

"To be a true *manō*, it's not all that tough.
Just swim around proudly and show off your stuff.
When fish are afraid, they'll respect you. It's true.
Just eat a few first. It is easy to do

Then they'll be quiet, our noisy *kaukini*.
All of your worries will seem so *manini*.
Plus fish are delicious, the healthiest treat.
I know that you'll like it. The taste can't be beat."

She pondered the words that she had been given.
Niuhi was the most cunning and driven.
“Perhaps I’m not trying as hard as I should.
Maybe eating iʻa would do me some good.”

She picked out a *moi*
and made her decision.
And took off with power,
grace and precision.

But just as she bore down
to capture her prize,
her tail stopped its thrashing
and tears filled her eyes.

"I'm such a failure. My *kaukini* are right.
I'm not a true *manō*, I don't have the bite."
She swam out for miles, far into the sea
and found a small reef that was bursting with glee.

A nanu was blowing his trumpet-like nose.
The pe‘a and wana were dancing in rows.
The *wai* was a dazzling aquamarine.
Glittering *i‘a* were a breathtaking scene.

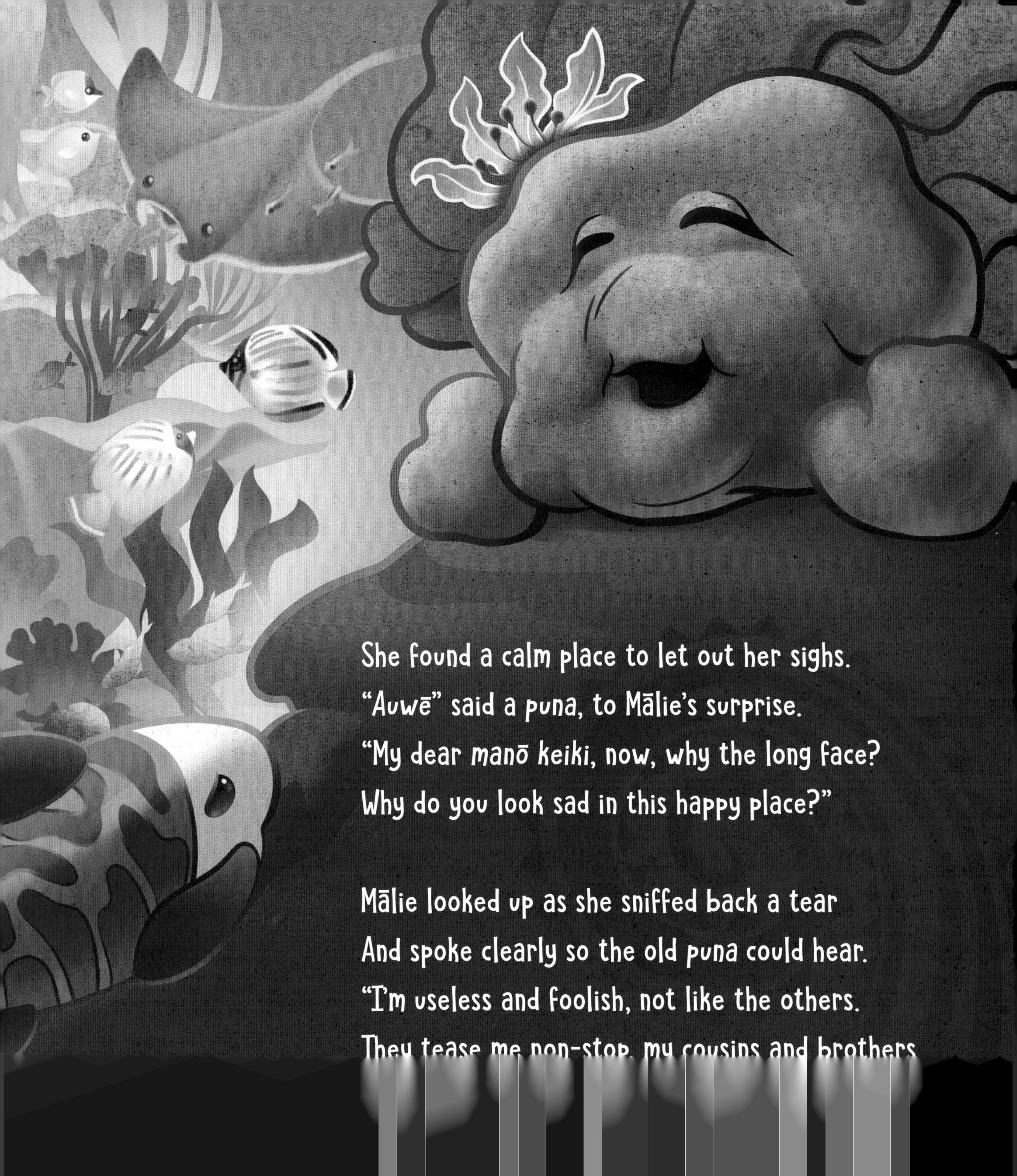

She found a calm place to let out her sighs.
"*Auwē*" said a *puna*, to Mālie's surprise.
"My dear *manō keiki*, now, why the long face?
Why do you look sad in this happy place?"

Mālie looked up as she sniffed back a tear
And spoke clearly so the old *puna* could hear.
"I'm useless and foolish, not like the others.
They tease me non-stop, my cousins and brothers

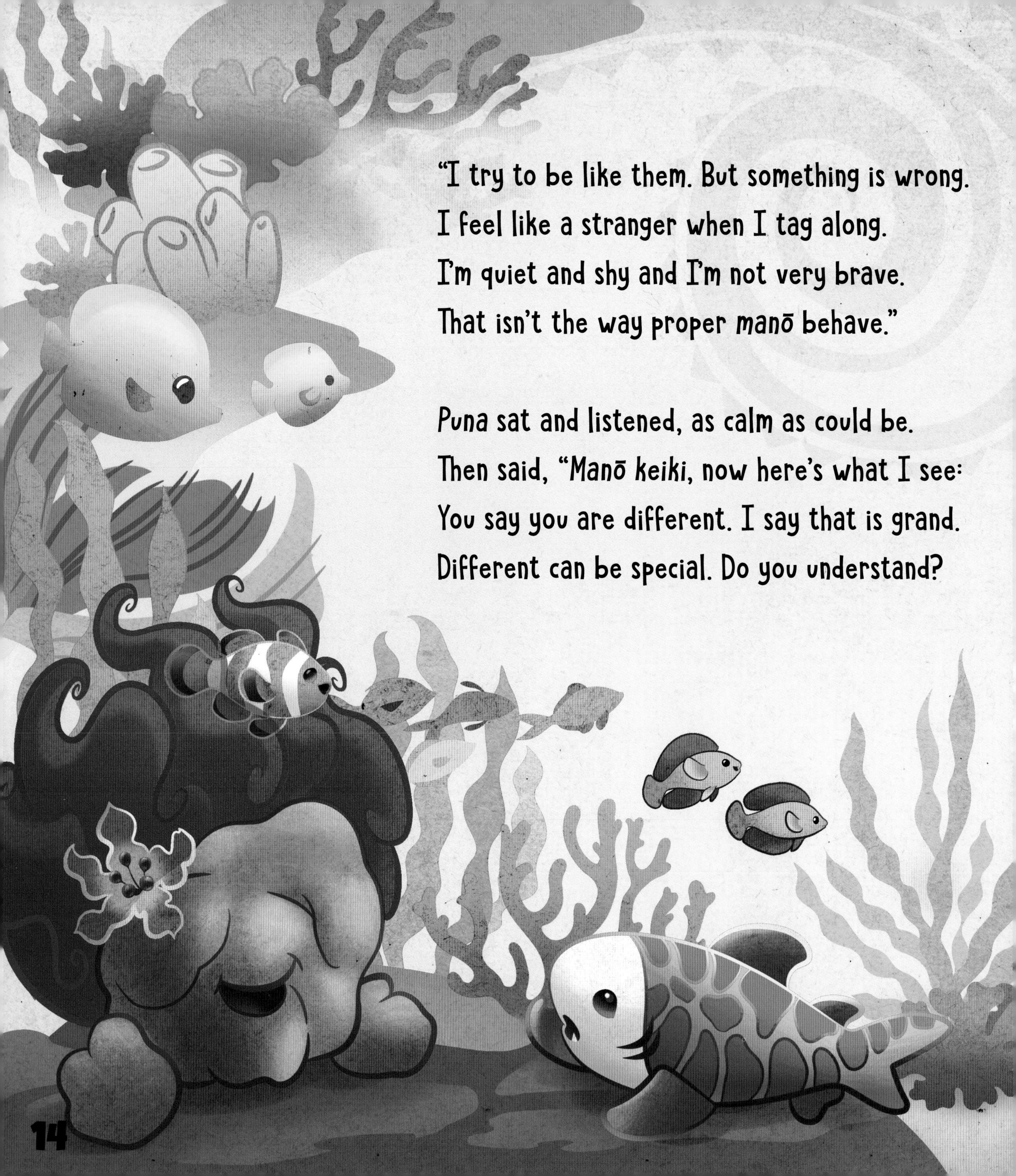

"I try to be like them. But something is wrong.
I feel like a stranger when I tag along.
I'm quiet and shy and I'm not very brave.
That isn't the way proper *manō* behave."

Puna sat and listened, as calm as could be.
Then said, "*Manō keiki*, now here's what I see:
You say you are different. I say that is grand.
Different can be special. Do you understand?

"If everyone did things in just the same way,
How would we grow ʻike and learn every day?
If the whole world was set and nothing could change,
How boring that'd be, no? How lifeless and strange.

You must have ideas, some thoughts all your own.
Use them and share them. Don't do it alone.
Some may laugh and tease you, but always stay true.
You said they are brave. But now, you must be too."

She thought for a moment and said, "You are right.
I'm still a true *manō* even if I don't fight.
I look before leaping, from thought, not of fear.
My strength can be kindness. Now it's all so clear."

She then thanked the *puna* and started to go,
To return to her waters. Her heart was aglow.
She'd found what she needed to make herself strong.
The strength was inside her and there all along.

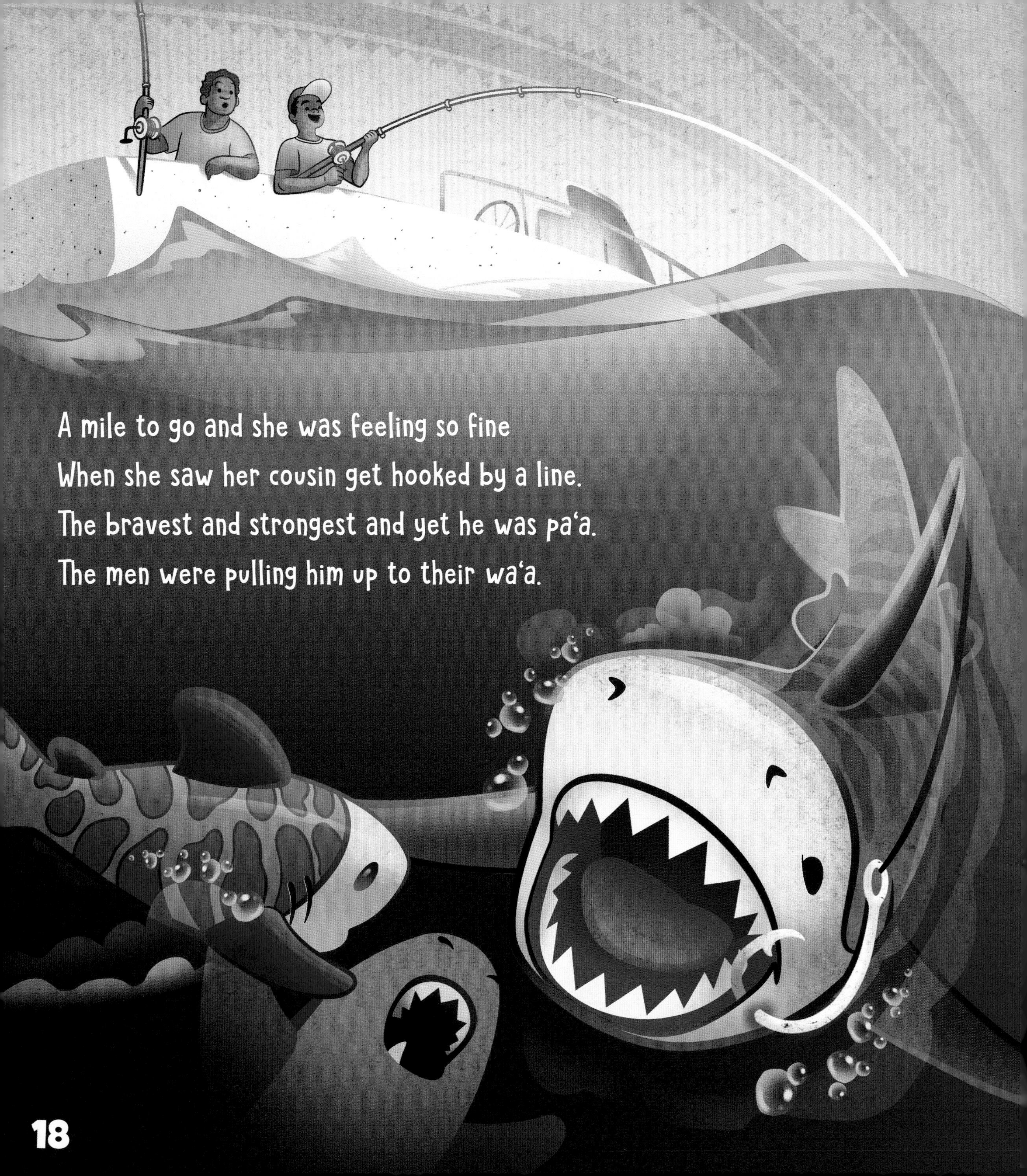

A mile to go and she was feeling so fine
When she saw her cousin get hooked by a line.
The bravest and strongest and yet he was *pa'a*.
The men were pulling him up to their *wa'a*.

The hook and the line were so hard to detect,
but Mālie saw it and zoomed there direct.
She bit through the line at a powerful rate
and saved her *kaukini* from his terrible fate.

Soon they were joined by her family and others,
Her father, her cousins and all of her brothers.
They saw how she helped without even blinking.
They all were impressed by Mālie's quick thinking.

Mālie then told them of all she had learned,
Of where she had gone and for why she'd returned,
Of power in kindness and wisdom in care,
Of value in her that she'd never seen there.

Her *Makua Kane* then parted the crowd.
His voice was powerful, though not very loud,
"My *keiki*, I'm sorry you struggled alone.
I wish I had seen it. I wish I had known.

But today you used your own special trait
to help out another and Dear, that is great.
From all that I've learned from life in the water,
None has been greater than this from my daughter."

So Mālie went home with her ʻohana
with a new ʻ*ike* of kindness and *mana*.
And though it's not always so easy to do,
she does what she feels her heart telling her to.

The End

GLOSSARY

Mālie	(mah-LEE-eh)	Quiet
Manō	(MAH-no)	Shark
Kaukini	(COW-key-nee)	Cousins; relatives
ʻOhana	(OH-hah-nah)	Family
Moi	(moh-EE)	A type of small fish
Mana	(MAH-nah)	Strength
Manini	(mah-NEE-nee)	Small
Iʻa	(EE-ah)	Fish
Nanu	(NAH-noo)	Trumpetfish
Peʻa	(PEH-Ah)	Starfish
Wana	(VAH-nah)	Sea urchin
Wai	(vI)	Water
Puna	(POO-nah)	Coral
Auwē	(OW-way)	An interjection, usually indicating surprise (Oh, Oh my, Goodness)
Manō Keiki	(MAH-no KAY-kee)	Baby shark; young shark
ʻIke	(EE-kay)	Knowledge; knowledgeable
Paʻa	(PAH-ah)	Stuck
Waʻa	(VAH-ah)	Canoe; boat
Makua Kāne	(mah-koo-ah-KAH-nay)	Father
Honu		Hawaiian green sea turtle
Kai		Ocean